Far Far Away!

by John Segal

Philomel Books

PHILOMEL BOOKS
A division of Penguin Young Readers Group.
Published by The Penguin Group. Penguin Group (USA) Inc., 375 Hudson Street, New York,
NY 10014, U.S.A. Penguin Group (Canada), 90 Eglinton Avenue East, Suite 700, Toronto,
Ontario M4P 2Y3, Canada (a division of Pearson Penguin Canada Inc.). Penguin Books Ltd,
80 Strand, London WC2R 0RL, England. Penguin Ireland, 25 St. Stephen's Green, Dublin 2,
Ireland (a division of Penguin Books Ltd). Penguin Group (Australia), 250 Camberwell
Road, Camberwell, Victoria 3124, Australia (a division of Pearson Australia Group Pty Ltd).
Penguin Books India Pvt Ltd, 11 Community Centre, Panchsheel Park, New Delhi - 110 017,
India. Penguin Group (NZ), 67 Apollo Drive, Rosedale, North Shore 0632, New Zealand
(a division of Pearson New Zealand Ltd). Penguin Books (South Africa) (Pty) Ltd,
24 Sturdee Avenue, Rosebank, Johannesburg 2196, South Africa. Penguin Books Ltd,
Registered Offices: 80 Strand, London WC2R 0RL, England.

Published simultaneously in Canada.
Manufactured in China by South China Printing Co. Ltd.
Text set in Berkeley Oldstyle.
The illustrations were rendered in pencil and watercolor on Arches 140 lb cold press paper.

Library of Congress Cataloging-in-Publication Data
Segal, John. Far far away / by John Segal. p. cm. Summary: When an unhappy young pig
decides to run away, his mother helps him to see that everything he needs and wants is right
there at home. [1. Mother and child—Fiction. 2. Runaways—Fiction. 3. Pigs—Fiction.]
I. Title. PZ7.S45258Far 2009 [E]—dc22 2008035855 ISBN 978-0-399-25007-1
1 3 5 7 9 10 8 6 4 2

For Emily and Josh.

Always, with love.

That's it.
I'm leaving.
Tonight. Forever.
You can't stop me.

Where are you going?

Away. Far far away from here!

Really?

YEAH.
I'm going.

Where?

I TOLD you already!

AWAY.

Far far away from HERE!

*How will you
get there?*

On my **BIKE.**

At night? You'll need a light.

Okay.

And your helmet.

Fine.

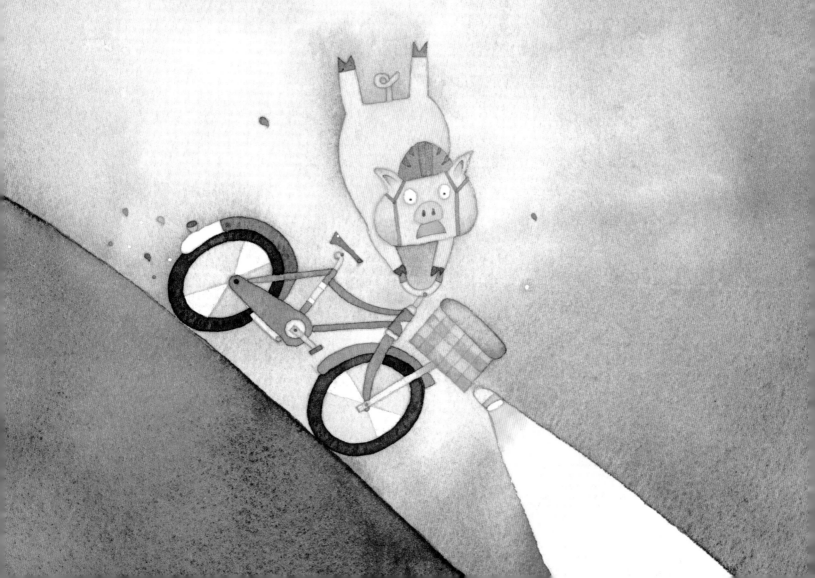

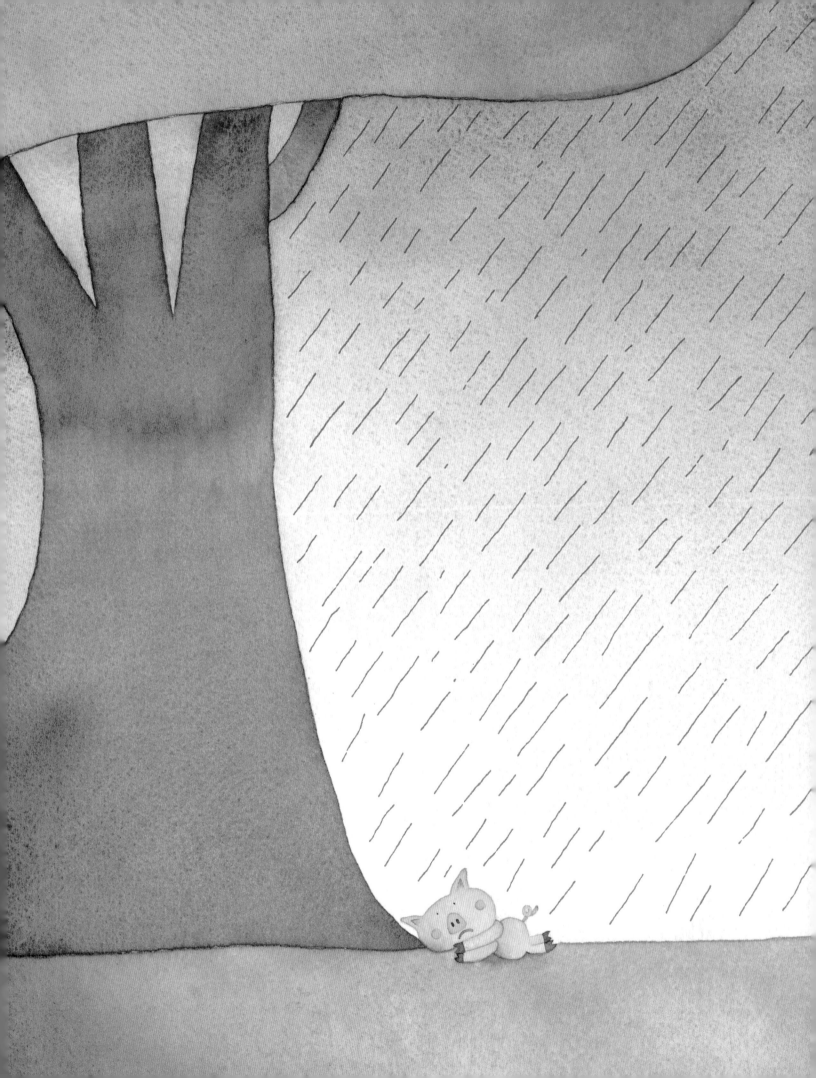

Where will you sleep?

On the **ground.**

And if it rains?

I'll get **wet.**

You might want to bring

a tent . . .

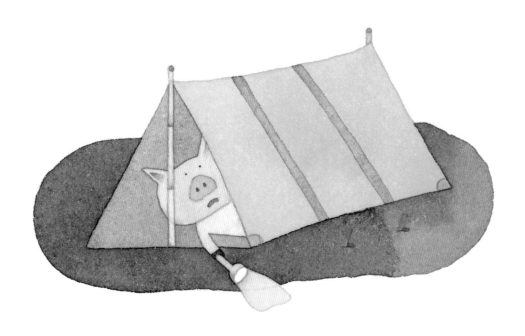

a sleeping bag . . .

a warm coat...

your blanky...

And Chester?

Yes, of course, Chester!

And Tiger?
And Max
and Rudolph, too?

Yes, of course, darling.

And Buttons...

and Race Car...

and Cowboy...

and Scout?

Why, of course!

Really?

Sure.

*Is there anything else
you want to bring…
maybe a piece of cake?*

CAKE?
There's cake?

*Yes, darling, but it's not done,
and you're all ready to go…*

Go?
**I'm not going
anywhere.**

**I have everything I need
right here.**

The End